Zip and

Episode Three:
Purple Planet

by Stan Cullimore

This is Blast. You may think that he is a post-box. But he is not! He is a shape-changing alien.

This is Zip. You may think that she is a lamppost. But she is not! She is a shape-changing alien, too.

Zip and Blast come from a purple planet far away.
They want to go back home but their spaceship is
broken.

3

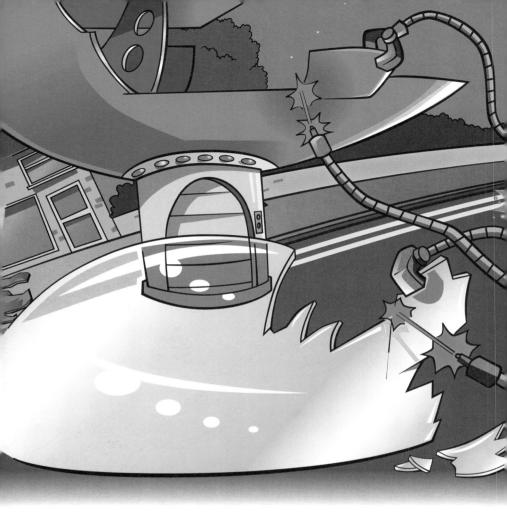

"Now what do we do?" asked Zip. "We will never get back to the Purple Planet in this spaceship."
Blast changed shape. He changed into a spaceship-mending robot. He began to mend the spaceship.
"Shall I help you, Blast?" asked Zip.

"No, thank you," said Blast.

"What shall I do then?" asked Zip.

"You could always work out how we are going to find our way back home," said Blast.

So Zip changed shape. She changed into a map-reading robot.

Zip pulled out a map of space. "I can't see a purple planet on this map," she said.

Blast sighed. "That is because you are wearing space sunglasses. They make all the colours change."

Zip took off the space sunglasses. "There is the Purple Planet!"

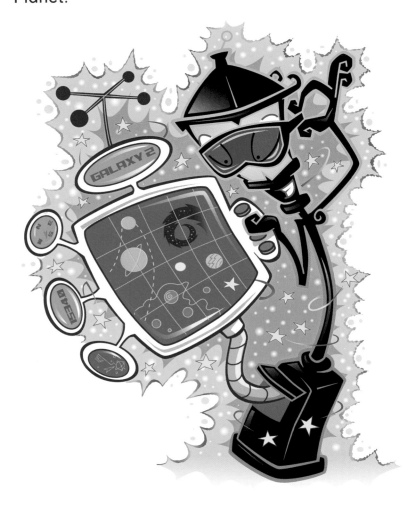

Blast smiled. "I've mended the spaceship," he said. He pressed a green button on the spaceship. A door opened. Blast changed into a post-box (he liked being a post-box). Zip changed back into a lamppost (she liked being a lamppost).

The two shape-changing aliens climbed into their spaceship. They sat down.

"4 – 3 – 2 – 1," said Blast.

"Blast off!" shouted Zip. "I do love saying that!"

She put on her space sunglasses.

Blast pressed a big pink button.

The spaceship flew up into the air. It shot across the sky. Zip looked out of the window. The Earth was a small planet far away.

"Which way do we go?" asked Blast.

Zip looked at the map. "I think it's that way," she said. "Turn left."

Blast pressed a yellow button.

The spaceship began to move. Soon it was going fast. Very fast. It was going so fast that all the stars began to look like white lines across the dark.

"The Purple Planet should be coming up soon," shouted Zip. She looked out of the window. "There it is."

Blast put his foot on the brake. The spaceship began to slow down. After a few seconds it stopped. They slowly floated down to the planet.

"Here we are," said Zip. "Back home on the Purple Planet."

The two shape-changing aliens got out of the spaceship. They went for a walk. Blast looked around. "But this planet is not purple. It's orange." Zip shook her head. "Don't be silly. The Orange Planet is where the big-mouth aliens live."

Blast stopped. "Big-mouth aliens?"
Zip nodded. "That's right."
"But they eat shape-changing aliens," cried Blast.
Zip nodded again. "Yes, they do."
"What is that over there?" asked Blast.

Zip took off her space sunglasses and looked.
"I think it's a big-mouth alien," she said.
"And what is that beside it?" said Blast.
"Another big-mouth alien," replied Zip.
The two shape-changing aliens looked at each other.
"HELP!" they shouted.

Zip and Blast changed into running robots.
"I don't want to be eaten," said Blast.
"Nor do I," said Zip.
Then they ran all the way back to the spaceship.

They jumped into the spaceship and lifted off.
"Which way do we go now?" asked Blast.
Zip put on her sunglasses and looked at the map.
"Turn right," she said.
Blast pressed a yellow button.

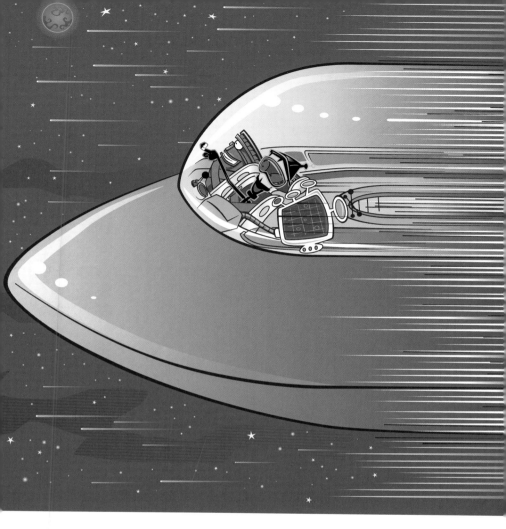

The spaceship began to move. Soon it was going fast.
Very fast. It was going so fast that all the stars began
to look like white lines across the dark.
"The Purple Planet should be coming up soon,"
shouted Zip. She looked out of the window.
"There it is."

Blast put his foot on the brake. The spaceship began to slow down. After a few seconds it stopped. They slowly floated down to the planet.

"Here we are," said Zip. "Back home on the Purple Planet."

The two shape-changing aliens got out of the spaceship. They went for a walk. Blast looked around. "But this planet is not purple. It's green." Zip shook her head. "Don't be silly. The Green Planet is where the jumping aliens live."

Blast stopped. "Jumping aliens?"

Zip nodded. "That's right."

"But they jump on shape-changing aliens," cried Blast.

Zip nodded again. "Yes, they do."

"What is that over there?" asked Blast.

Zip took off her space sunglasses and looked.
"I think it's a jumping alien," she said.
"And what is that beside it?" said Blast.
"Another jumping alien," replied Zip.
The two shape-changing aliens looked at each other.
"HELP!" they shouted.

Zip and Blast changed into skipping-out-of-the-way robots.

"I don't want to be jumped on," said Blast.

"Nor do I," said Zip.

Then they skipped all the way back to the spaceship.

They skipped into the spaceship and lifted off.
Blast looked at Zip.
"I know why we keep on going to the wrong colour planet," he said.
"Why?" asked Zip.
"Because you are wearing those stupid space sunglasses," shouted Blast.

Zip nodded. "You are right. They make all the colours change!"

"We have to find the Purple Planet," said Blast.

Zip looked at the map. "I don't know which way to go next," she said.

Blast closed his eyes and pressed a green button.

The spaceship began to move. Soon it was going fast.
Very fast. It was going so fast that all the stars began
to look like white lines across the dark.
"There is a planet just ahead," shouted Blast.
"Yes, I can see it," shouted Zip.

Blast put his foot on the brake. The spaceship began to slow down. After a few seconds it stopped. They were floating in space.

"Where has the planet gone?" asked Blast.

"Over there," said Zip. She pointed out of the window. There was a planet beside them.
"What colour is it?" asked Blast. "And remember to take your sunglasses off before you look!"

Zip took her sunglasses off and looked out of the window. "It's purple!" she shouted.

The spaceship slowly floated down to land on the Purple Planet.

The two shape-changing aliens got out of their
spaceship.
"I am so glad we got back home – at last," said Blast.
"So am I," said Zip.

Blast looked at Zip.

"Zip," he said slowly. "I've got a good idea."

"What is it, Blast?" asked Zip.

"Let's never, never, NEVER leave the Purple Planet – ever again," said Blast.
"That is a really, really, REALLY good idea," said Zip.